This

PLAYDATE KIDS

Book

belongs to:

_____

Chloe   Cosmos   Danny   Dakota

For my grandchildren Brian, Mary, Matthew, Seth, Owen and Clara
and to all the children I've helped for the past 34 years in Malibu, my hometown - A.T.

For Julian - W.M.E.

Copyright ©2006 Playdate Kids Publishing

PO Box 2785
Malibu, CA 90265-9998

ISBN 1-933721-02-2

Library of Congress Control Number 2006901345

Printed in China

Danny is Moving

by
Annie Thiel, Ph.D.

illustrated by
William M. Edwards

PLAYDATE KIDS PUBLISHING

LOS ANGELES

A TERA FANNING PUBLICATION

Danny's mom got a letter offering her a great new job.
She told Danny that they would have to move to a new town.

"But Mom, I don't want to move," Danny sighed.
"I like the way things are just fine."

"I like my house,
with all its familiar twists and turns."

"I like my yard
and I like my favorite tire swing."

"And I really like playing soccer with my friends!" Danny said.

Danny knew he had to move, but he didn't like it.
"I don't WANT to leave my friends, my school and my house,"
he told his best friend, Charlotte.
He was glad he had someone he trusted to talk with about his feelings.

Scared

Happy

Sad

Mad

Charlotte said, "When something big happens in our life, we have lots of different feelings about it. It's normal and okay to have all of these feelings."

At school, Danny made a special goodbye card
for all of his teachers. He thanked them for
teaching him so much, and told them he would miss them.

Danny said goodbye to all of his friends
at school. He promised to write them letters.
His best friend, Charlotte, said,
"I promise to write letters to you too, Danny!"

Moving day finally came.

Danny and his mom drove away.
"Goodbye old house!" he shouted.

When Danny got to his new house, he was feeling very sad.
His new house was okay, but he missed his old house,
his old school, and his old friends.

That night, Danny and his mom had a picnic supper
on the living room floor.
It was fun, but Danny was worried about his new school.
He used his words to tell his mom how he felt.
"I'm scared about school tomorrow, Mom," he said.

"New things can be scary, but they can also be fun and exciting,"
Mom replied. "I think school will be fun."

Danny was still scared the next morning.
"Mom! I changed my mind! I don't want to go!" he cried.
"I don't know anybody!"

"It's okay, Danny. Just remember to be yourself,
talk to the other kids, and everything will work out fine,"
his mom said.
"Anyone would be lucky to be your friend!"

At school, the teacher introduced Danny to the class.
Danny felt nervous.

Danny was put into a group with kids he didn't know.
Nobody talked to him at first.
They were all nervous, too.

Danny remembered that his mom told him
to talk to the other kids if he wanted to make friends.
"Hi, I'm Danny. I like playing soccer," he said.

At school, Danny still missed his old teachers.

But his new teachers were nice, too.

At home, Danny still missed his tire swing
in his old backyard.
But he found something even better in his new backyard.

Danny still missed his old room.
But he liked that after school he could
see who was playing outside.

He still missed playing soccer with his old friends.
But Danny also had fun playing soccer with his new friends,
Chloe, Cosmos and Dakota.

Danny knew that he would always
miss his old friends...

...but he also knew that he had made new friends.

New friends. Old friends. Lots of friends.
There is always room for more friends!

Things to Remember When You Move

1. You can still write letters to your old friends, and call them when you miss them.

2. It's okay to feel scared, or nervous about moving to a new place.

3. Talk to someone you can trust about your feelings.

4. Ask lots of questions about the place where you are moving.

5. Even though you will miss your old friends, you can make lots of new friends.

6. Try to talk to the new kids in your class. They are nervous about meeting you too.

7. Don't worry if you don't make new friends right away—sometimes it takes a while to get used to new people and become friends with them.

8. Ask your parents to help you make lots of playdates with your new friends.

9. Tell your parents how to make your new room special, just for you.

10. Moving to a new place and a new house can be very exciting!

Draw a picture of your new house.

MORE THE PLAYDATE KIDS BOOKS
LET'S BE FRIENDS!

Chloe Nova
Chloe gets a new baby brother!

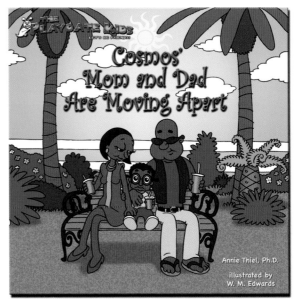

Cosmos McCool
Cosmos' parents get a divorce.

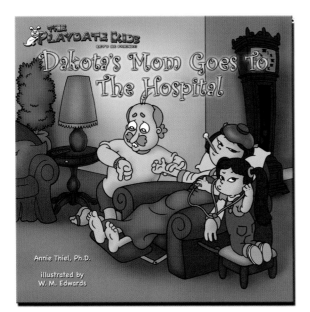

Dakota Greenblatt
Dakota's mom goes to the hospital.

The Playdate Kids
Behavioral themed
coloring and puzzle book
AND animated cartoon DVD set!